Enid Blyton's

TELL-A-STORY BOOK

The Enchanted Umbrella and other stories

The Clever Kitten

COSY was a little tabby kitten, five months old. She was called Cosy because she always looked such a cosy bundle when she curled herself up on a cushion.

She lived upstairs in the nursery, and the children made a great fuss of her. But Mother said she must soon be a kitchen cat and go and catch mice in the the larder.

The children were upset. They did so love having Cosy in the nursery. Sometimes she slept in the doll's cot, and often she went out for a walk wheeled in the doll's pram.

"Mother! If you make her live in the kitchen she will grow fat and lazy and won't play any more!" said Lucy. "Oh, please, do let her belong to us and be the nursery cat."

But Mother didn't seem to think it would be a

good idea at all. So Cosy was told that for one week more she could be a nursery kitten—and then she must go downstairs and become a kitchen cat.

Now, one afternoon Cosy had a shock. She was sitting upstairs in the nursery armchair, dozing, wondering if she should get up and try and catch a fly that was buzzing round the table when she suddenly saw somebody looking right in through the window.

Cosy jumped and spat. She arched her little striped back and hissed at the face that looked in at the window. She knew who it was. It was the garden-boy, Alfred, who had sometimes caught her and pulled her tail. And now here was Alfred staring in at the nursery window. Whatever was he there for?

The nursery was upstairs. Cosy wondered if Alfred had suddenly grown legs long enough to reach to the nursery. It was most extraordinary. She didn't know that Alfred was standing on a ladder. He had been sent up to tie a big branch of the climbing rose-tree that had got loose.

Alfred stared into the nursery. The cupboard door was open, and in the cupboard Alfred saw things that made his mouth water. There was a bag of sugar lumps. A tin of biscuits stood there too. A bottle of sweets was next to it. A slab of chocolate was near by. Goodness! Alfred thought it was marvellous to see so many good things together.

He looked down into the garden. Nobody was there. He peered carefully into the nursery. Nobody was there either.

"I'll chance it!" said Alfred to himself. "I could get all those things into my pocket!"

Now as Alfred climbed in at the window, he pushed the ladder, quite by accident, and it fell to the ground below! And there was Alfred in the nursery, with no ladder to get down again by! He would have to go down the stairs.

Cosy the kitten glared at him. She didn't like the unkind garden-boy at all. She spat and hissed at him. He threw a brick at her from the brick box and it hit Cosy on the tail. The kitten leapt out of the chair and flew at Alfred. She scratched him down the hand. Oh, if only, only she could make someone come and catch this bad boy before he took all the things out of the cupboard!

And then Cosy had a marvellous idea! The nursery piano was open. She had often seen Lucy playing on it, making all kinds of noises, deep and loud, and high and tinkly. Perhaps Cosy could make a noise on it too, and then someone might hear and come to the nursery!

So Cosy leapt up on to the open piano and ran up and down the black and white keys. "Ping, ping, pong, dingle-dingle, doom!" went the keys, making a funny little tune of their own.

Cosy was rather frightened. It was funny to make noises with her feet. But she went on and on running up and down the piano, though Alfred threw another brick at her to make her get off!

Now Mother was sitting in the room below, reading. She knew that Nurse and the children were out. And when she heard the strange noise going on upstairs she couldn't *imagine* what it was!

She jumped up and listened. "Ping, ping, pong, dingle, dingle, DOOM!" went the noise. The loud, deep DOOM sound was the lowest key on the piano.

"It's someone banging about on the nursery piano!" said Mother, in great astonishment. "Whoever can it be?"

She ran upstairs to see—and when she got to the

10

nursery, what did she find but Alfred stuffing his pockets full of sugar lumps and sweets and biscuits! And there was Cosy still on the piano, playing the keys by running up and down, up and down!

"ALFRED!" said Mother. And how Alfred jumped! In two minutes he was downstairs, and the gardener was telling him just exactly what he thought of him, and just what happened to bad boys who climbed in at other people's windows and stole. What a shock for Alfred!

But how thrilled the children were when they came home and heard all that had happened!

"Clever little Cosy!" cried Lucy, picking up the

11

purring kitten. "Mother, don't make her into a kitchen cat, please, please, don't! Why, she can even play the nursery piano! And she has saved all our biscuits and sweets and sugar. Mother, do let her belong to the nursery always and always!"

"Very well," said Mother, with a laugh. "You can have Cosy for your own. But do teach her to play the piano properly, my dears, because although the noise she made was very good for catching a thief, I wouldn't at all like to hear it going on all day long!"

So Lucy is going to teach Cosy to play the piano properly. Do you think she will be able to?

The One—Eyed Rabbit

THERE was once a toy rabbit who had two beautiful glass eyes. He could see very well indeed with them, and so it was a dreadful shock to him when he lost one.

They were stuck very tightly into his head, not sewn on like the teddy-bear's. Sometimes the teddy-bear's eyes came loose and then they were wobbly, and everyone laughed at him till somebody sewed them on properly again.

The rabbit was soft and cuddly, and had a white bobtail at the back, and a beautiful pink ribbon round his neck. He was a jolly, kindly fellow, always being asked out to parties by the pixies who lived in the daffodil-bed below the nursery-window. He used to ask the curly-haired doll to iron out his pink ribbon for him whenever he went out. He did like to be neat and pretty.

Well, one day the dreadful thing happened. Janet took the rabbit, the curly-haired doll, and the teddy-bear out into the garden with her—but when she came in again, she forgot all about the rabbit.

She put the curly-haired doll into her cot, and

popped the teddy-bear into his corner of the toy-cupboard. The bear put his head out of the cupboard as soon as the little girl had gone out of the room, and called to the doll.

"I say, Curly-haired Doll, is the rabbit left out in the garden?"

"Yes—isn't it dreadful!" said the doll, sitting up in her cot. "What are we to do? Could you go and get him, do you think? He'll never find his way back to the nursery by himself."

"I'll have to wait till the night-time, then," said the bear. "Somebody might see me if I go running out into the garden now."

So when night came, the bear slipped out of the window, climbed down the apple-tree outside, and ran to the garden seat where Janet had played with him and the doll and the rabbit that morning. It was pouring with rain, and the bear was really very worried about the rabbit.

The rabbit was sitting on the seat, miserable, wet, and cold. He didn't like to jump down by himself because the seat was rather high. He was *so* pleased to see the bear.

"Oh, you *are* nice to come and fetch me," said the rabbit joyfully. "Can you help me down from this high seat, Teddy?"

"Of course," said the bear, and he held out a plump brown paw. The rabbit jumped, and landed on the grass. He rolled over, but he didn't hurt himself at all. Then, taking the bear's paw, he hurried up the wet garden to the apple-tree, climbed to the window, and was soon safely inside the nursery being petted and fussed by all the toys.

And then as he sat drying himself by the fire, the curly-haired doll noticed a dreadful thing. The rabbit only had one eye! His left eye wasn't there!

15

."Oh, Rabbit!" She squealed in alarm. "Where's your left eye? It's come off! Did you know?"

The rabbit put up his paw and was dreadfully upset when he found that he only had one eye. "I thought I couldn't see very well," he said. "The rain must have wetted it, and it came unstuck and fell off. Oh, dear, oh, dear—how very, very dreadful!"

The bear at once climbed out of the window and went to look for the lost eye in the garden. But he couldn't find it at all—which wasn't very surprising, because a worm had already found it and taken it down his hole. So the poor bear came back without the eye.

The rabbit sat by the fire and wept big tears out of his one eye. "I look dreadful," he said. "I shall never go out to parties any more. I shall never go out to tea. No one will want a horrid one-eyed rabbit. I shan't even go for a walk again. And I don't expect Janet will love me any more, now I've only got one eye."

"Don't be so silly, Rabbit," said everyone, but the rabbit just wouldn't be comforted. He wept and wept and wept.

Then the bear had a marvellous idea. He jumped up and ran to the toy-cupboard. He came back with Janet's new box of glass marbles. They were very beautiful and she was proud of them.

"Look, Rabbit," he said. "We may be able to find a nice blue glass marble that matches your right eye—and if we saw it in half, we can stick it into your head, and then you will have two eyes again and can be happy!"

"But what will Janet say when she finds one of her marbles in half?" cried the rabbit.

"Well, as she was careless enough to leave you out in the rain, she deserves to lose half a marble," said the bear. And all the toys nodded and said he was right.

They soon found a marble that was exactly the

right blue. They had to call in one of the pixies to saw it in half, because none of the toys knew how to, and it needed a little magic to saw neatly through the glass of the marble.

The bear put one half back into the box of marbles. Then he found a tube of glue and squeezed some on to the flat side of the half-marble. Then he cleverly pressed it into the right place on the rabbit's head.

"Hold your new glass eye there till it's stuck," he told the rabbit. So the rabbit held it, and then, when it was properly stuck, he took his paw away, and there he was with two lovely blue eyes again.

"Oh, you look even nicer than before!" cried all the toys in delight. "Can you see all right, Rabbit?"

"Yes—it's a fine eye," said the rabbit joyfully, gazing all round the nursery with it. "Better than my other one. Thank you, Teddy, for being so clever."

He looked fine, though the marble eye was just a bit bigger than his other eye. But nobody minded that, and as for the rabbit, he never even knew. He was so pleased and happy that he did a little rabbit-dance all round the nursery and back again, and the toys sat and clapped him.

What will Janet say when she finds that one of her lovely marbles is cut in half? Do you think she will guess what has happened when she sees her rabbit's odd eye?

18

The Ball that Vanished

JENNY and Fred had a beautiful big rubber ball. It was bright blue one side and bright red the other side, and when it rolled along quickly it wasn't blue or red, but purple instead.

"It goes purple when it rolls because the blue and the red mix up together and make purple!" said Jenny, who knew quite a lot about painting.

They played every day with the big blue and red ball. They rolled it, they kicked it, they threw it, they bounced it. It didn't mind a bit what they did with it. It just loved everything.

And then one day it vanished. It really was rather extraordinary, because neither Jenny not Fred saw where it went.

They were having a fine game of "Throwing-the-ball-over-the-house". I don't know whether you have ever played that game, but if your house isn't too high it is rather fun. One of you stands at the front of the house, and the other one stands at the back, and you can only do it if Mother says you may. Anyway, Mother said that Fred and Jenny might play it till dinner-time.

So Fred stood at the back and Jenny stood at the front. Fred threw the ball high into the air and it went right over the house. Jenny saw it coming over the chimneys and she gave a shout of joy. She held out her hands for it, and it dived right into them.

"I've caught it, Fred!" she cried. "Look out—it's coming back to you!"

She threw it up into the air—but she didn't throw it hard enough, and it struck the tiles, rolled down the roof, and fell back into her hands again. She threw it once more, and this time it sailed right over the top. Fred gave a shout.

"I see it! It's coming! Good throw, Jenny. I've caught it!"

Then Fred aimed that ball high again and up it went over the house once more. But Jenny didn't call out that it was coming. There was no sound from her at all.

"Jenny! Have you caught it?" shouted Fred.

"No. It hasn't come yet," said Jenny, puzzled. "Did you throw it? Did it go right over the roof?"

"Of course," said Fred. "Didn't you hear me shout? It *must* have fallen your side, Jenny. Look for it."

So Jenny looked all over the front garden, but not a sign of that big blue and red ball did she see. It was most annoying. Fred came running round to the front.

"Haven't you found it yet?" he asked. "Jenny, you don't know how to look!"

"I *do!*" said Jenny crossly. "I've looked everywhere. It's you that doesn't know how to *throw*. The ball must have fallen back into your half of the garden. I shall go and look there!"

So Fred hunted in the front garden and Jenny hunted in the back one. But neither of them could find that ball. It really had completely vanished. It was very queer.

They went in and told Mother. "Could a ball disappear into the air?" asked Fred.

"Of course not," said Mother. "It's a pity if you have lost that nice ball. It really was a beauty."

Well, that wasn't the only unpleasant thing to happen that day. When the children went into their nursery to look for another toy to play with, they found the room full of smoke.

"Mother, Mother, the house is on fire!" said silly Jenny, with a scream. But Fred knew better.

"It's the chimney smoking!" he cried. "Mother, come and put the fire out in the grate. The smoke is coming out into the room."

Mother hurried in, vexed and worried. How she did hate to see all the smoke pouring out into the nursery and making it black and dirty!

"I can't imagine why it is doing this," she said, vexed. "The sweep only came a few weeks ago, and usually this chimney goes at least six months without cleaning. Oh, dear—it's no good. I must ring the sweep and tell him to come. Some damp soot must have stopped up the chimney."

So the sweep came with his brushes, and the children watched him in delight. Sweeping a chimney seemed a most glorious thing to do, and both Jenny and Fred made up their minds that when they were grown-up they would spend at any rate a little time of their lives being chimney-sweeps.

The sweep put a brush up the chimney, and then fitted another pole to the brush-handle. He pushed that up the chimney too. Then he fitted on another pole and pushed that up as well.

"You see, Jenny, all these long poles push the brush higher and higher up the chimney, sweeping as it goes, till it comes to the top!" said Fred in delight.

"Does the brush come right out of the top of the chimney?" asked Jenny.

"Of course," said the sweep, his black face smiling at them, showing very white teeth. "You run outside into the garden, Missy, and shout to me when you see my old black brush poking itself out of the top of your chimney! Then I'll know it is right out and I won't fit on any more poles!"

So out went Fred and Jenny and watched the

22

nursery chimney. And soon Jenny gave a scream of joy.

"Look, Fred, look! The brush is just coming out!"

Sure enough, something was coming out of the chimney. It was the sweep's brush—but on top of it was something round and black and queer. Whatever could it be?

"What's that on top of the brush?" said Fred. "Is it a black stone, do you think? I'll go and tell the sweep."

So into the house he ran and told the surprised sweep that there was something on top of his brush.

"A bird's nest, maybe," said the sweep. "Birds sometimes build their nests in a chimney, you know, and that stops it up and makes it smoke. I'll come and look."

So the sweep left his long poles standing upright in the grate, and went out to look. He stared and stared at the thing on top of his round brush, and then he went back indoors again.

"I'll shake and wriggle my poles so that the brush throws off that thing, whatever it is," he said. "I really don't know *what* it can be."

So he shook his poles and the brush shook too —and off came that round black thing, bounced all the way down the roof and fell into the garden!

And it was—yes—you've all guessed right! It was the children's big ball, very black, very sooty, and very sorry for itself indeed!

"Oh! It's our ball!" shouted Fred, picking it up and making his hands all sooty. "Oh, Jenny—it fell down the chimney when I threw it up! And it stopped up the chimney and made it smoke! It must just have fitted the chimney-pot!"

Jenny was excited and pleased. "Let's wash it," she said. "Won't Mother be surprised!"

So they washed the ball, and it came all clean and blue and red again. But it never bounced quite so high as it used to, because the chimney had been hot, and the ball had been nearly cooked.

And now the children don't like to play "Throw-the-ball-over-the-house" in case it pops down the chimney again! Mother says it really costs her too much to look after a ball that is so fond of chimneys. Now, pray, don't throw *your* ball down a chimney too!

The Elf in the Nursery

JUST outside the nursery window there was a climbing rose-tree. It was very old, and had a thick twisted trunk, and hundreds and hundreds of leaves. In the summer it blossomed out, and was red with sweet-smelling roses.

In one of the thickest parts of the climbing rose lived a small elf called Lissome. She was a dear little thing with two long wings rather like a dragonfly's, which made a whirring noise when she flew.

Lissome was lonely, for no other elves lived in the garden. They were afraid of the two children who lived in the house. They were twin girls called Lucy and Jane, and they were rough and rude. So no elves lived near them, except Lissome, who felt quite safe from them, high up in the climbing rose.

All the same it was a lonely life there. The

sparrows sometimes came and talked to her. The robin had a song for her, and sometimes the summer butterflies and bees fluttered round and told her the news.

When she discovered that there were toys in the nursery who came alive at night and played merrily with each other, she was simply delighted!

She peeped in one night at the window and they all saw her!

"Look! An elf!" said the golliwog. "Let's ask her in!"

So in she flew on her long wings and smiled at all the wondering toys. There were the golliwog, the brown bear, the blue rabbit, three dolls, the black dog, the brown dog, and the pink cat. So there were a good many folk to play with!

Every night Lissome went to play in the nursery. All the toys loved her, for she was merry and kind. They played hide-and-seek, and catch, and hunt the slipper, and hunt the thimble, and a great many other games, too—the kind you play when you go to a party.

"You are lucky to be able to fly out of the window at dawn," said the golliwog one night. "We wish we could too!"

"Why?" said Lissome in surprise.

"Well, Lucy and Jane are such rough children," said the brown bear. "Look at my arm! It's almost off! The two children both wanted to play with me today, so they pulled and pulled—and my arm nearly came off! Whatever shall I do when it does?"

"I *am* sorry," said Lissome.

"And look at my tail," said the pink cat. "Lucy twisted it and twisted it today—and that's nearly off too. It may drop off at any minute! And who wants a cat without a tail?"

"You know, Toys, if you could lend me a needle and cotton, thimble and scissors, I think I could mend you," said Lissome. "I'm quite good at sewing."

"Are you really?" said the golliwog joyfully. "Well, here is Nurse's work-basket. It's got a lot of sewing things in it. Take what you want."

So Lissome took out a thimble which, however, was far too big, so she couldn't wear it. She took a tiny needle and threaded it, and she found a pair of scissors. Then she set to work.

She sewed the bear's arm beautifully. He was very pleased.

"It feels as firm as ever," he said, swinging it to and fro. Lissome took the scissors and snipped the cotton.

"Now I'll do the pink cat's tail," she said. The pink cat at once turned round backwards, and Lissome threaded the needle with pink silk to sew on the tail.

Now the golliwog had been watching everything with great interest. He couldn't sew— but he did wish he might use those scissors! Snip, snip, they went, and he wished he could make them go snip, snip, too!

"Let me snip the cotton next time," he begged. So Lissome said he might. He picked up the scissors and put them ready. He snip-snipped them in the air just to practise using them—and then a dreadful thing happened!

He snip-snipped the scissors too near Lissome the elf—and she stepped back just at that moment —and the golliwog snipped off one of her lovely wings!

"Ooooooh!" cried Lissome in fright. She turned round and saw her lovely wing on the floor. The

golliwog burst into sobs. He was terribly upset and unhappy.

"Forgive me, forgive me!" he wept. "I didn't mean to. Oh, what shall I do, what shall I do?"

"You wicked, careless golliwog!" cried the pink cat, who saw how pale the elf had gone. "Just when Lissome is doing a kind turn to us you go and snip off one of her beautiful wings!"

"I didn't mean to, I tell you—I didn't mean to!" howled the golliwog, more upset than he had ever been in his life before.

Lissome patted him gently. "Don't cry so," she said. "It was an accident."

"But what will you do?" wept the golliwog. "You can't fly now."

"Well, I must just stay in my rose-home until my wing has grown again," said the elf.

"Oh, will it grow again?" cried everyone joyfully. Nobody had thought of that.

"Of course," said the elf. "It will only take a week. So cheer up Golly."

He did cheer up. He squeezed out his wet hanky and tried to smile. Then something else came into his mind, and he looked miserable again.

"*Now* what's the matter?" said the elf.

"I've just thought—you can't fly out of the window tonight," said the golliwog. "So what will you do?"

"Oh, dear," said the elf. "I hadn't thought of that. Can I climb up somehow?"

"No. There's nothing to climb on," said the pink cat. "There's no chair by the window, and we are not big enough to put one there. Golly—use your brains. You got Lissome into this muddle. Now get her out of it! Go on—use your brains, if you've got any, or we'll all be very angry with you."

The golly thought hard. "We'll hide her!" he said.

"Don't be silly," said the brown bear. "You know that the nursery is turned out tomorrow. There won't be a single corner that isn't swept."

"Put her in the brick box," said the brown dog.

"Yes—and let Lucy and Jane find her if they use their bricks tomorrow!" said the pink cat scornfully. "And if they treat *us* roughly, what do you suppose they will do to a little elf like Lissome? They would make her *very* unhappy!"

"The brick box has given me an idea!" said the golliwog suddenly. "Let's get all the bricks out — and build a high castle up to the windowsill! Then Lissome can walk up the bricks and climb out to her home!"

"Now that really *is* a good idea!" said the brown bear, and he went to the big brick box. He and the golly emptied out the bricks on the floor, and then all the toys began to build a high castle to the window-sill.

It took ages, because the toys were not very good at building, and the bricks kept tumbling down. But at last the castle was done, and just reached the sill!

"It's dawn now!" whispered Lissome, and she climbed up the bricks. "You must sleep, or you will be seen running around. Thank you for your help, Toys! I'll come again when my wing has grown."

The toys heard someone moving about downstairs. Someone was up! They scuttled into the toy-cupboard and shut the door. "We've left the bricks out!" whispered the golly, and he lay quite still in a corner. "Oh, dear!"

Well, there wasn't time to put them back into the box, for Lucy and Jane were now both awake, and dressing. They rushed into the day nursery—and *how* astonished they were to see the bricks leading up to the window-sill!

"Who's built that?" said Lucy.

"And what for?" said Jane.

"The *toys* can't have done it!" said Lucy. "How I'd like to know what it's there for!"

But she never did know. As for the elf, her wing grew again in seven days, and she fluttered in at the window once more, as merry as ever. But she wouldn't let the golliwog use the scissors again — and I'm not surprised, are you?

The Poor Little Owl

IN the field nearby lived a little brown owl. John and Betty often saw it sitting on the telegraph wires in the dusk, when they went to bed.

"Tvit, tvit, tvit!" said the little owl to them, and the children called "Tvit, tvit!" back to it. It wasn't very big, and when it spread its wings it flew very silently indeed.

Then one evening, as John and Betty walked home, they saw the little owl disappear into a hole in an old, old willow tree.

"I guess it has got its nest there!" said John in excitement. "I wonder if there will be any baby owls. We must watch and see."

But before they knew, a sad thing happened to the little owl. It went to drink from the pond one night, overbalanced, fell into the water and couldn't get out! So in the morning John and Betty

33

found that it was drowned, and they were very sad.

"Oh, John—what about the baby owls, if there are any in the tree?" said Betty in tears. "There won't be anyone to feed them. They will starve to death, poor things."

John spoke to the gardener about the nest he was sure was in the old willow tree. "Couldn't you look and see if there are any baby owls there?" he said. "We don't want them to starve, you know."

"I'm not going after any owls," said the gardener at once. "Dangerous creatures they are, with their sharp claws! My goodness, even a baby owl can get its claws into you so hard that you can't get them out. Torn to pieces your hand would be!"

"Oh," said John. He went away, but he kept on and on thinking about the owls. He felt sure they were hungry and unhappy.

"Betty, there must be *some* way of getting them out," he said. "Do think. You're clever at thinking."

So Betty thought. "Well," she said, "if their claws are so sharp and strong that they can dig right into your hand and not let it go, what about letting down something into the nest—a handkerchief, perhaps—and letting them dig their claws into that. Then all we need to do is to draw up the handkerchief and the owls will come too!"

"Marvellous idea!" cried John. And so it was. Betty borrowed a big old silk hanky from Daddy's drawer, and the two children went to the old willow tree. They climbed up it and came to the hole, which went deep into a thick branch of the tree.

A faint hissing noise came up from the hole. "Goodness—is there a snake in there?" said Betty.

"No! Owls do hiss, you know," said John. "Now, Betty—where's the hanky? Hand it over."

John took the hanky and let one end slowly down into the hole. There were two baby owls in the tree. They turned themselves over so that their clawed feet were on top—and how they attacked that silk hanky! They dug their feet into it and their claws caught in the silk.

"Got them nicely!" shouted John, and he pulled up the hanky. There were the two fluffy baby owls holding on to it for all they were worth! John popped them into a box he had brought with him, shut the lid, and then switched his torch on to see the nest.

"There isn't really any nest," he called to Betty, "just a few shavings from the hole, that's all. But wait a minute—what's this?"

The light of his torch had shone on to something red. John put his hand into the hole and felt what it was. It seemed to be a little bag of some sort. He pulled at it—and it came out. It was heavy.

"Betty! The owl had made her nest on top of this little bag!" cried John. "Look—it's got the name of the bank on it. I do believe it's the bag of gold that a thief stole from the bank messenger last winter! He must have hidden it here and then forgotten where the hiding place was!"

"Goodness!" said Betty, as John opened the little red bag and a whole heap of shining golden coins winked up at them. "What a lot of money! Come and tell Mother."

Well, that was a most exciting afternoon. The children had two baby owls for pets, and a bag of gold to give back to the bank! And what do you think? The bank manager gave the children one of the pieces of gold!

"That's your reward," he said. "Buy what you like with it."

So what do you think they bought with the money? They went to the shops and bought a marvellous cage in which to bring up their two pet owls! It was painted blue outside, and had red perches inside, and was very grand and big indeed.

"You can keep your little owls there and bring them up in safety till they are big enough to fly away and look after themselves," said Mother. "You must feed them well, give them fresh water, and clean out their cage every single day."

So they did, and soon the two owls grew tame and friendly, and sat peacefully on the children's fingers whenever they were held out to them. Betty and John were very proud of their pets, because no one else at school had owls; and even the teacher came to see them, and said what strange and curious birds they were.

"They look rather like little feathered cats!" she said. And so they did, as they sat side by side on their perches, their big golden eyes looking solemnly at the visitor.

And now they have flown away to look after themselves; but John and Betty have left the cage door open in case they might like to come back there to sleep. I expect they will sometimes.

Every night the two little birds call to their friends and say "Tvit, tvit, tvit!" from the nearby field. I wonder if *you* have heard them. They call so sharply and so loudly that I shouldn't be a bit surprised if you hear them too!

Conceited Clara

CLARA was a doll—and goodness, what a marvellous doll she was! She wore a blue silk frock, a wonderful coat to match; blue shoes and socks, and a hat that was so full of flowers it looked like a little garden.

It was the hat that everyone admired so much. There were daisies, buttercups, cornflowers, poppies and grass round the hat, and it suited Clara perfectly. She knew this, so she always wore her hat, even when she played games with the toys.

"You are vain, Clara!" said the golliwog teasingly.

That made Clara go red. She *was* vain, and she knew she was pretty. She knew that her clothes were lovely. She knew that her flowery hat was the prettiest one the toys had ever seen, and that it made her look really sweet.

38

"I'm not vain!" said Clara. "Not a bit!"

"You are! You're conceited and stuck-up," said the teddy-bear, who always said what he thought. "Why, you even wear your hat when you play with us. And if we play a bit roughly you turn up your nose and say, 'Oh, please! You'll tear my pretty frock!' Pooh! Conceited Clara!"

Clara was angry. She glared at the bear and then she walked straight up to him. She took hold of his pink bow and tugged at it. It came undone, and Clara pulled it off. And then she tore the ribbon in half. Wasn't she naughty?

"Oh! You horrid doll! Look what you've done! You've torn my ribbon and now I can't tie it round my neck, and I shall show where my head is sewn on to my body," wept the bear.

"Serves you right," said Clara, and she walked off.

Well, after that the toys wouldn't have anything to do with Clara. They wouldn't play with her. They wouldn't talk to her. They wouldn't even speak when she called to them. So Clara was cross and unhappy.

One night, when the children were asleep and the toys came alive to play, Clara took her beautiful flowery hat and hung it up in the dolls' house. She thought perhaps the toys might play with her if she didn't wear her hat. She fluffed out her curly hair and gazed at the golliwog.

"Ho!" said the golly. "Now you want to show off

39

your curly hair, I suppose! Well, go and show it to the fender and the coal-scuttle and the poker! *We* don't want to see it, Conceited Clara!"

So that wasn't any use. Clara went to a corner and sulked. She was very angry. How dare the toys take no notice of her, the prettiest doll in the whole nursery!

Then the toys planned a party. It was the birthday of the clockwork mouse, and everyone loved him because he was such a dear. So they thought they would have a party for him and games, and give him a lovely time.

But they didn't ask Clara. The teddy cooked some exciting cakes and biscuits on the stove in the dolls' house, and the golliwog cut up a rosy apple into slices. The toys set out the chairs round the little wooden table and put the dishes and plates ready.

Everything looked so nice. "It's a pity that we can't put a vase of flowers in the middle of the table," said the golly. "I always think flowers look so sweet at a party. Come along, everyone—we'll just go and tidy ourselves up and then the party can begin."

They all went to find the brush and comb in the toy-cupboard. Clara peeped from her corner and thought that the birthday-table looked lovely with its cakes and biscuits and apple-slices.

"I do wish I had something to give the clockwork mouse," thought Clara. "I do love him. He's such

a dear. But I expect he would throw it back at me if I had anything to give. The toys are all so horrid to me now."

And then Clara suddenly had a marvellous idea. What about her flowery hat? Couldn't she take the flowers off that beautiful hat and put them into a vase for the middle of the birthday-table? They would look really lovely.

She rushed to get her hat. She tore the flowers from it. She found a dear little vase, and began to put them in—buttercups, daisies, cornflowers, poppies and grass. You can't think how sweet they looked.

Clara popped the vase of flowers in the middle of the table and went back to her corner. She looked at her hat rather sadly. It looked very queer without its flowers. She would look funny if she wore it any more.

The toys ran to the birthday-table to begin the party—and how they stared when they saw the lovely flowers in the middle of the table!

"Where did they come from?" cried the golly in astonishment.

"Oh, what a lovely surprise for me!" cried the clockwork mouse. And then he guessed who had put the flowers there for him.

"It's Clara! They are the flowers out of her hat!" he squeaked. "Oh, Clara, thank you! Do, do come to my party!"

"Yes, do come!" cried all the toys. And the golly ran and took her hand.

"If you can give up the flowers you were so proud of, you can't be so horrid after all!" he cried. "Come along, Clara, and join the party."

So Clara went, and everyone was so nice to her that she was quite happy again. Sometimes she wears her hat without the flowers, and do you know what the toys say? They say, "Why, Clara, you look just as nice without the flowers—you really do!"

And so she does!

The Enchanted Umbrella

ONE day, when Kathleen and Morris had gone to look for blackberries in Cuckoo Wood, they had a strange adventure. It all began because of the rain.

The sun had been shining out of a blue sky when they started out, but when they were deep in the heart of the wood, picking great big blackberries, the sky clouded over.

"Isn't it getting dark!" said Kathleen, looking up at the black sky between the trees. "I'm afraid it's going to pour with rain!"

Just as she spoke the rain came—and how it poured! The children huddled under a thick tree and watched in dismay.

"We haven't our mackintoshes with us," said Morris, "nor even an umbrella! We ought to have taken a satchel with us and put our raincoats in, in case. Now we shall get soaked!"

They stood under the tree, gazing at the pouring rain. The tree dripped and dripped; everywhere was as wet as could be.

Then suddenly Kathleen stared at something in astonishment, and pointed. "Look!" she cried. "What's that against the tree over there? Is it an umbrella? No, surely it can't be!"

Morris looked, but he couldn't see the umbrella. Kathleen suddenly darted out from beneath the tree to fetch it.

"I don't know who it belongs to,!" she cried, "but we'll use it to shelter us until the rain has stopped. It looks a lovely big one."

Morris stood under the tree and watched Kathleen run to a beech tree not far off—and there, sure enough, leaning against the trunk was a bright green umbrella with red spots on it! Kathleen ran to it, picked it up and opened it. It was very large indeed, big enough for three or four people to get underneath.

And then a very strange thing happened. Just as Kathleen began to run back to Morris with the green umbrella, she stopped and looked puzzled.

"What's the matter?" called Morris.

"The umbrella is pulling at my hand," said Kathleen—and, as Morris watched he could quite plainly see that the umbrella was pulling hard at Kathleen. Then he knew that it was magic, and he shouted to Kathleen.

"Let it go! It's enchanted! Let it go, Kathleen!"

"I can't, I can't!" shouted poor Kathleen in a fright. "The crook handle has taken hold of my hand and it's pulling me along!"

Kathleen was certainly being pulled along, away from Morris. He started to run over to her, but as soon as the umbrella heard him it pulled at Kathleen's hand all the more strongly, and off she went with it, running at top speed between the trees! The umbrella was very clever at dodging the branches, and although Morris ran as hard as he could through the rain, he couldn't catch it.

Soon he had lost sight of it, and he stopped in dismay. Now what was he to do? He *must* find Kathleen somehow! He couldn't let a strange umbrella go off with her like that. He looked round him. He was in another part of the wood, where he had never been before.

"Now I'm lost!" he said. "Oh, goodness, what a dreadful morning!"

Soon he spied a small cottage set under a great oak tree. "I'll go there and ask my way," he thought. He was just about to walk towards the cottage when he heard the sound of someone running through the wood, and to his great surprise he saw a small gnome, with long pointed ears and a long nose. Morris have never seen any of the little folk before, though he knew they lived in Cuckoo Wood, and he stared in astonishment.

The gnome was crying loudly, and tears dripped off his nose like raindrops. He ran up the path and banged on the door of the little cottage. Someone opened it, and the gnome began to talk loudly.

"I stood your umbrella by the old oak tree whilst I went to call on my mother!" he wept. "I was only gone a minute and when I came back it had disappeared! Yes, it was quite gone. Oh, dear, I'm so sorry! It was so kind of you to lend it to me, and now I've lost it! Where do you suppose it has gone?"

"Hi, hi!"shouted Morris, running to the cottage in excitement. "I can tell you about that umbrella!"

He ran up the pathway to the little door, hoping that the gnome would help him to get Kathleen back safely. The little gnome stared at him in surprise. At the door stood a brownie with a long beard.

"Come in, both of you," he said. "It's still raining. There's no need to get wet!"

Morris went inside. It was a queer little place, dark and full of furniture. He soon told the gnome what had happened when Kathleen had found the umbrella, and the little man's face became longer and longer as he listened.

"My goodness!" he said dolefully. "Who would have thought the umbrella would behave like that?"

"Well, it's an enchanted one, you know," said the brownie. "It used to belong to Dame Twiddle-pins, who lives on the top of Sugar Hill—I expect it's gone back to her!"

46

"But what about Kathleen?" asked Morris, in dismay.

"Oh, she's gone too," said the brownie. "That used to be an old trick of that umbrella's, when it was young—taking people off to Dame Twiddle-pins. She was half a witch in those days and lived in a great shining palace. She was always wanting people to help her with her spells, so she used to let her umbrella fetch them for her."

"Poor Kathleen!" said Morris. "Whatever shall I do? Which way is it to the Sugar Hill?"

"Good gracious, you're not thinking of going to Dame Twiddle-pins, are you?" said the brownie.

"Of course I am," said Morris. "I must rescue Kathleen somehow."

"I'll come with you," said the gnome. "You would never be able to find the way by yourself."

"Oh, thank you," said Morris, gratefully. "We'd better start now. It's stopped raining."

The brownie went to the door and saw them off. The gnome took Morris through the trees until he came to a very tall one.

"We climb up this," he said. Morris looked at it. He liked climbing trees, but this one was very difficult. It was soaked with rain and was green and slippery.

The gnome swung himself up on a branch and began to climb—but in a second he was down again, his nice red suit all covered in green.

"We'll have to go up inside," he said. "I'll just knock and see if it's convenient."

To Morris's surprise he knocked on the tree with a little wooden knocker that looked like a knob of bark. A small door opened in the trunk and an old lady looked out.

"What do you want?" she asked. "If you're selling scissors, I don't want any today."

"We're not selling anything," said the gnome, politely. "We just want to know if you'd mind us using your stairs inside the tree today. It's so slippery outside."

"All right," said the old woman. "But see that you wipe your feet!"

They stepped inside the big tree and wiped their feet carefully on the mat. Morris was astonished to see that he was in a hall. An open door looked into a cosy kitchen with a bright fire. Two other doors were shut. A spiral stairway was in the middle of the tree, and the gnome led the way up this.

"This tree belongs to old Mrs. Acorn," he said. "She lets all the rooms in it to lodgers. We shall pass their doors as we go up."

Morris was more and more astonished. They went up the staircase, and as they passed each landing he looked at the doors. Some had brass plates on them, with printed names. "Frisky Squirrel" was on one plate, "Mister Fiddlesticks" on another. Morris wondered what he could be like.

As they passed one door it opened and a small pixie looked out. "Oh," she said in disappoint-

49

ment. "I thought you were the washing coming." Before Morris could say anything she had shut the door.

They went up and up, passing many rooms on the way. At last the tree narrowed until there was only room for the stairway. Then that ended in a small platform and Morris, and the gnome came out at the very top of the tree.

Morris stepped on to the platform and looked round. He was right at the very top of the wood! The tree they had climbed was higher than any other, and Morris could see far down below him the green, waving tops of the other trees.

"Where do we go now?" he asked.

"We must wait for the Cloud Bus," said the gnome, picking acorns off the top of the tree, and throwing them down through the branches. Morris felt excited. The Cloud Bus! Whatever could that be like? He watched for it, and very soon saw a queer-looking carriage bumping along over the clouds. It seemed to be made of clouds itself, and was painted all the colours of the rainbow. It came rolling to the top of the tree, and stopped at the platform. Its wheels were set with misty wings, and it was these that sent it along.

"Get in," said the gnome. Morris stepped in half-frightened, for really, the bus didn't look strong enough to hold him. But it was! He sat down on a seat and looked round. There were only two other passengers, a man in a pointed hat who looked like a wizard, and a very stiff-looking rabbit dressed in a black coat and a high collar, with a shiny top-hat on his head. His ears stuck out at each side and made Morris want to laugh, but the rabbit looked so solemn that he didn't like to.

The conductor came to give them tickets. The gnome gave him two pennies, which, to Morris's surprise, were green instead of brown, and asked for Sugar Hill.

"Sorry," said the conductor, who was a small brownie with his beard tucked neatly into his belt. "We don't go there, you know. The nearest we go is Sleepy Town."

"Well, we'll go there, then," said the gnome. "I don't *want* to," he said to Morris, "because it's a dreadful place to get out of. It's so difficult to find anyone who will tell you the way."

The bus went on through the air, the little wings on the wheels flying and making them go round. The next stop was Tip-up Corner. Morris thought it a very good name for whatever place it was, for the bus tipped up and he and the other two passengers all went sliding to the front. The rabbit's top-hat came off and he was very much upset. He went after it and fell right out of the bus. Morris saw him tumbling down through the air.

"He's all right," said the conductor. "He nearly always gets out like that. Sleepy Town's the next stop. I'll put you down in the market-place."

The bus went on to Sleepy Town. It flew down-

wards for a change and Morris saw that it was on the ground again, its wheels still moving by means of the little wings. Soon it came to a quiet, sleepy-looking village and stopped in the market-place.

"Here you are," said the conductor. "Sleepy Town!"

They got out and looked round. There were a few stalls in the market, but under the big umbrellas that protected their goods from the sun, the people of Sleepy Town sat, fast asleep. They were round, fat little people, with button noses and shiny cheeks. Morris felt sleepy himself when he looked at them. He yawned loudly. The gnome looked at him in alarm.

"I say, don't do that!" he said. "If you once go to sleep here, you might not wake up for months."

"Good gracious!" said Morris, alarmed. "I'll be careful, then."

"The thing is—which way do we go to Sugar Hill?" said the gnome. "If only we could find someone to ask! They are all sound asleep!"

"Wake them then!" said Morris. He went up to a small fat boy who sat fast asleep against a wall, his mouth wide open. Morris shook him. Then he shook him again. All that happened was that the boy shut his mouth, and began to snore.

"It's no good," said the gnome, watching. "You never *can* wake anyone up in Sleepy Town. If we could find the fire-bell we might be able to. That's about the only thing they listen to!"

"Come on, then, let's find it," said Morris. So they looked up and down the crooked little streets —and at last Morris found the fire station! Inside was a bright and shining fire-engine—and by it,

53

hanging on the wall, was a great fire-bell.

"Good!" cried Morris. He ran to it, took it down and rang it. Goodness, what a clanging it made! The gnome almost jumped out of his skin—and then, in the same minute he cried: "Look out! The fire-engine is moving!"

Morris looked round and saw the fire-engine rushing towards him all by itself. He had no time to get out of the way, so he quickly jumped up on the front of it with his bell. The gnome jumped on too, and off they both went down the street on the swift fire-engine!

But the streets were no longer sleepy. Everyone had awakened as if by magic! They jumped up, they came rushing out of the houses, they shouted loudly. When they saw the fire-engine they were more excited than ever.

"Where's the fire?" they called, to the gnome and Morris. This was awkward. There was no fire, of course. Morris thought it was better not to answer that question. Instead he asked another.

"Which is the way to Sugar Hill?"

"Oh, is that where the fire is?" shouted the fat little folk. "Down to the right, across the river, and you'll see Sugar Hill in the distance. Hurry there and we'll follow and help you to put the fire out!"

The gnome began to laugh when he saw the round Sleepy Town folk jumping on bicycles, and getting into carts and cars to find out where the fire was. "We've woken them up all right," he said. "I

54

say, how do you guide this fire-engine? We must make it go the right way."

It didn't seem to need any guiding at all. It rushed to the right, round a corner, and thundered towards a river that shone in the distance. It rolled over a wide bridge, and then Morris and the gnome saw, glittering in the distance, a curious hill, as white as snow. On the top stood a small house which looked as if it might topple over at any moment!

"There's Sugar Hill!" said the gnome, pleased.

On went the fire-engine, and as it came near Sugar Hill Morris saw that it was unwinding long hoses.

"Look!" he said to the gnome. "The engine really thinks there's a fire!"

"And look behind you!" said the gnome. "The whole of Sleepy Town is coming after us!"

So it was! Hundreds of the little fat folk were coming along in crowds, eager to see where the fire was. Morris began to wonder what they would say when they knew there was no fire!

The engine stopped at the foot of the white sugary hill. Morris and the gnome jumped off. They began to climb the hill, slipping backwards every now and then in the snow-like sugar. When they reached the top they looked at the strange house that rested there. It really looked as though a good strong push would send it down to the bottom of the hill on the other side!

Outside the door stood the enchanted umbrella, green, with red spots! Morris gave a shout when he saw it, and so did the gnome. So Kathleen was here after all! Good!

Morris was going to knock at the door when the gnome stopped him. "Don't do that," he whispered. "If old Dame Twiddle-pins comes she'll be angry to see that we've brought half Sleepy Town with us, and she'll whip us. Peep in at the window."

So Morris crept to the window and peeped inside the house. The first thing he saw was Kathleen sitting in a corner, crying. She was trying to sew a great checked duster with a coarse, blunt needle, and it was dreadfully hard work. The tears fell on the duster, and Morris felt very sorry for Kathleen. Then he saw Dame Twiddle-pins, nodding, half-asleep, in a rocking-chair. If only he could make Kathleen see him!

He tapped gently on the window, and then bobbed down in case the old woman should look up and see him. Then he heard a deep voice speaking, the voice of Dame Twiddle-pins.

"Go to the window, girl, and look out. It sounds as if a bird is tapping at the pane. It may be my pigeon. Let it in."

Kathleen went to the window and opened it. As soon as she leaned out she saw Morris crouching underneath. He beckoned to her to jump out of the window, and at once she did so, delighted to see her brother. He dragged her down to him and then they crept round to the other side of the house, where the gnome was.

"Oh, Morris!" said Kathleen, in joy. "I knew you'd rescue me! That horrid old woman has set me to do all sorts of nasty, hard jobs for her, ever since that umbrella brought me here, and she wouldn't let me go home."

Just then there was any angry shout from inside the house.

"Girl! Where are you? Come back at once or I'll come and fetch you."

Morris, the gnome and Kathleen crouched together on the other side of the house. The old dame ran to the door and stood there, looking for Kathleen—and at that very moment the fire-engine filled its long hose with water, held it up like an elephant's trunk and squirted a great jet all over Dame Twiddle-pins! She gave a loud scream of surprise and fright and fell backwards into the kitchen, soaked through. She went to the open window, shouting with rage, and the engine squirted water through that too. Then up the hill came climbing all the little fat folk of Sleepy Town, carrying buckets of water, and what a time they had!

They flung their water everywhere, and soon the inside of the house was dripping wet. Dame Twiddle-pins was quite beside herself with rage and amazement, for she couldn't imagine what every-

one was doing—and at last, so fierce and angry was she that the Sleepy Town folk stopped and listened to her.

"How dare you, how dare you!" shouted the old dame, shaking her stick at them.

"We came to put out the fire," said one of the fat folk.

"I didn't have a fire!" shouted Dame Twiddle-pins.

"But a boy rang the fire-bell and started the fire-engine off here," said another.

"Oh, that's someone come to get the girl I had here then," said Dame Twiddle-pins, in a rage. "Well, find them. They must be somewhere about. The hill's too steep to get down at the back and we should have seen anyone climbing down the front!"

Morris, Kathleen and the gnome wondered whatever they were going to do. They were still hiding at the back of the house. The gnome suddenly stood up and grinned. "I've thought of something!" he said. "Wait here for me!"

He slipped round the side of the house to the front door. Everyone was most astonished to see him, and no one tried to capture him at all. They just stood with their mouths and eyes wide open in surprise!

The gnome caught up the green umbrella, dashed round the house with it and opened it. He hooked it on to his belt, held out a hand to each of the two children, and shouted suddenly in a very loud voice, "Home, Umbrella!"

The umbrella immediately tugged hard at the gnome's belt and began to take them down the hill at the back. It was very steep, but with the help of the umbrella and the gnome, the children managed all right. Everyone came running round to the back of the house, Dame Twiddle-pins too, and how they shouted to see the three escaping.

"You woke us up, you bad boy!" cried one of the Sleepy Town folk, shaking his fist.

"You took our fire-engine," roared another.

"You've spoilt my house!" screamed Dame Twiddle-pins.

"Good-bye, good-bye, see you another time!" called the gnome, cheekily, as they all reached the bottom of the hill. The umbrella took them swiftly along. It seemed to know its way marvellously well. In less than ten minutes it was back in Cuckoo Wood, dodging between the still wet trees in a very clever manner.

It stopped outside the brownie's house and the

gnome unhooked it from his belt. The brownie opened his door and looked out. The umbrella walked into his kitchen and put itself into a small umbrella-stand there. It really was a marvellous umbrella!

"So you're safely back!" said the brownie. "Well, come in and have a cup of cocoa. I've got some made for you. Then you, gnome, can take the children home."

So they all went in and drank hot, sweet cocoa, and told the brownie their queer adventures. When he heard about the people throwing water over Dame Twiddle-pins he laughed till he cried.

"That will serve her right!" he said, wiping his eyes. "She's a hard, mean old creature, and that will teach her a lesson! Oh, dear, oh, dear, how I wish I'd been there!"

"I think it's time we went home," said Morris, at last. So they said good-bye to the brownie, promised to go and see him again, and went with the gnome, who saw them safely to the edge of the wood. Then off they ran home, longing to tell their mother all that had happened.

But she thought that they had made it all up—so tomorrow they are going to take her to the brownie's house in the wood, and show her that strange and surprising thing—the brownie's enchanted umbrella!